Bird Hotel

Written by Jill Eggleton
Illustrated by Richard Hoit

 Rigby

Mrs. Biddle lived by herself.

"I like to live by myself," she said.

One day, Mrs. Biddle looked out of her window and she saw birds everywhere.
They were making nests in her tree and they were chirping.

"Go away!"
Mrs. Biddle shouted.
"I want to live by myself."

But the birds stayed
in Mrs. Biddle's tree,
and they chirped all day.
Mrs. Biddle stayed inside.
She was not happy!

When spring came,
the birds chirped
and chirped.
"What a noise!"
said Mrs. Biddle.
She looked out of
her window and saw . . .

baby birds in every nest!

The mother birds flew
in and out of the tree . . .

with worms

and bugs

and grubs.

They flew in and out
of the tree all day long.

"This is terrible,"
shouted Mrs. Biddle.
"There are too many birds
in my tree. I just want
to live by myself."

But poor Mrs. Biddle
couldn't live
by herself.

People came to
Mrs. Biddle's house
to look at the birds.

Buses stopped
by her house
and people took
photographs.
Kids came and sat
under the tree.

"This is terrible,"
said Mrs. Biddle.
"I just want to live
by myself."

Then one day,
Mrs. Biddle woke up
and she couldn't hear
the birds.
There were no birds
in the tree
and no birds
in the nests.
There was
no chirping.

Mrs. Biddle
looked at the sky
and she saw
snow clouds.
"Winter is coming,"
said Mrs. Biddle.
"Those birds
have gone away.
Good! Now I can live
by myself."

Winter came.
Mrs. Biddle
missed the people
stopping by her house.
She missed the people
taking photographs.
She missed the kids
sitting under her tree.

And . . .

she missed the birds!

So Mrs. Biddle made a sign
and she put it on the tree.

> Bird Hotel
>
> Vacancy

Then one day,
spring came.
Mrs. Biddle woke up
and she heard chirping.
She looked out of her window
and she saw birds everywhere.
"Good," said Mrs. Biddle.
"The birds are back.
I didn't like living by myself!"

A Flow Diagram

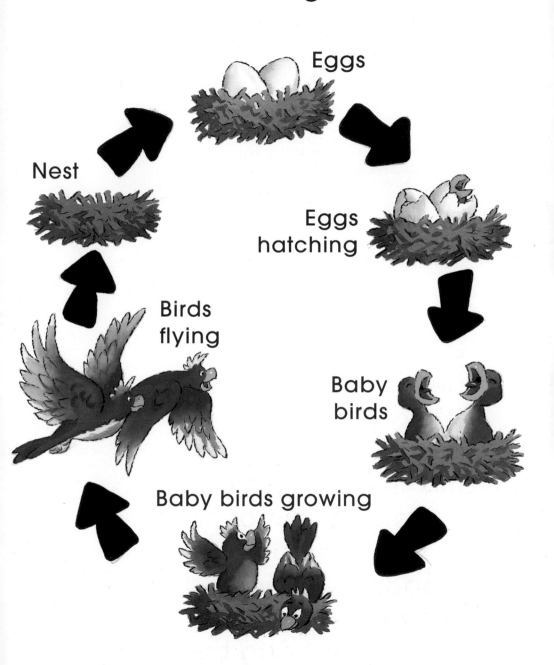

Eggs

Eggs hatching

Baby birds

Baby birds growing

Birds flying

Nest

Guide Notes

> **Title: Bird Hotel**
> **Stage:** Early (4) – Green
>
> **Genre:** Fiction
> **Approach:** Guided Reading
> **Processes:** Thinking Critically, Exploring Language, Processing Information
> **Written and Visual Focus:** Flow Diagram, Sign

THINKING CRITICALLY
(sample questions)
- What do you think this story could be about?
- Look at the cover. What do you think is unusual about the tree?
- Look at pages 4 and 5. Why do you think Mrs. Biddle looks unhappy?
- Look at pages 8 and 9. Why do you think all the people are at Mrs. Biddle's place?
- Look at pages 10 and 11. What could Mrs. Biddle be thinking?
- Look at pages 12 and 13. How do we know Mrs. Biddle wants the birds back?
- Look at page 14. Why do you think Mrs. Biddle changed her mind about the birds?

EXPLORING LANGUAGE

Terminology
Title, cover, illustrations, author, illustrator, title page

Vocabulary
Interest words: chirping, chirped, terrible, vacancy
High-frequency word (new): those
Compound words: myself, herself, photographs, everywhere

Print Conventions
Capital letter for sentence beginnings, title, names (**M**rs. **B**iddle) and signs (**B**ird **H**otel **V**acancy), periods, exclamation marks, quotation marks, commas, ellipses